This book belongs to

_____

_____

For Dennis, Christine, Mark, Elsie and Jim . . .
C.A.

First published in Great Britain in 2009 by
Gullane Children's Books
185 Fleet Street, London, EC4A 2HS
www.gullanebooks.com

10   9   8   7   6   5   4   3   2   1

Text and illustrations © Claire Alexander 2009

The right of Claire Alexander to be identified as the author and illustrator of this work
has been asserted by her in accordance with the Copyright, Designs and Patents Act, 1988

A CIP record for this title is available from the British Library

ISBN: 978-1-86233-648-3 hardback
ISBN: 978-1-86233-758-9 paperback

Printed and bound in Indonesia

Small
Florence

CLAIRE ALEXANDER

GULLANE
CHILDREN'S BOOKS

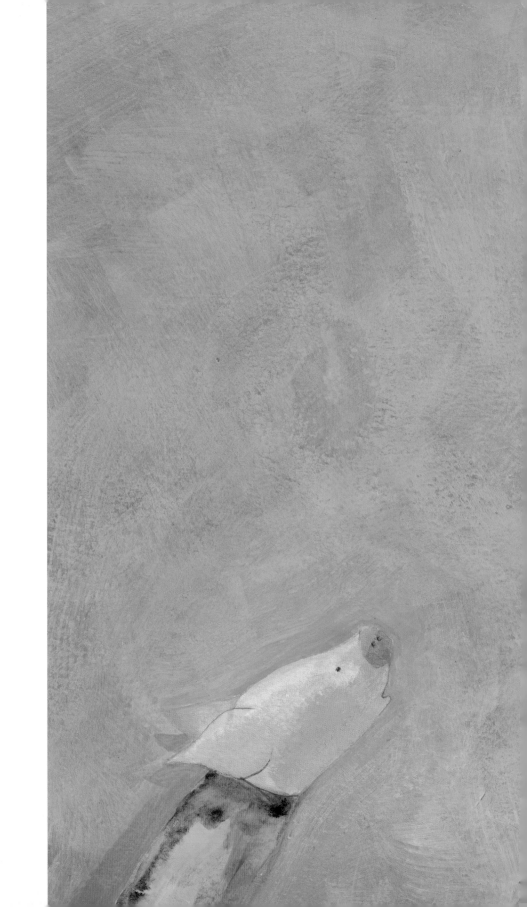

Florence was a small pig.
She was a happy soul,
if a little shy at times.

She had two older sisters.

"What's small, pink and squeaky?"

"Florence!"

Florence thought her sisters were very lucky. They were taking singing lessons from Jazzy-Funk Mutt, the cool singing teacher.

"Ham it up, Sisters! Smooth!"

Florence dreamed of
one day becoming a piggy
pop star on television.

She sang to herself in secret. She sang
under the covers of her bed at night and
she sang in the bath every morning.

After a while, she plucked up the courage to sing to her friends...

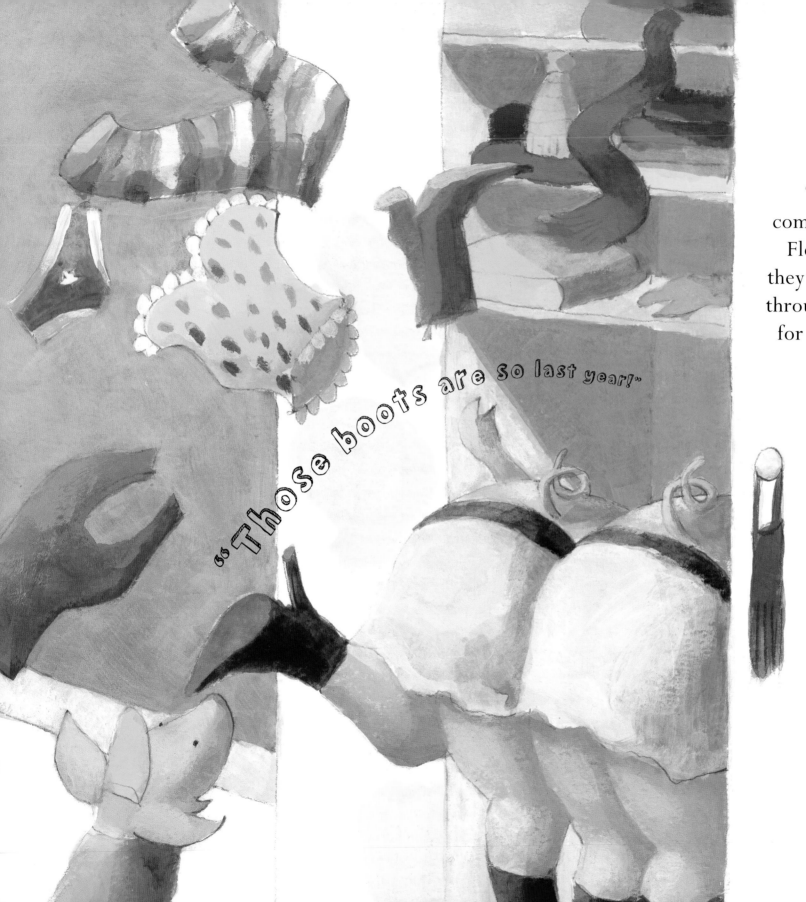

"Those boots are so last year!"

"Let's enter the competition!" squealed Florence's sisters as they started rummaging through their wardrobes for costumes to wear.

"Can I sing with you in the competition?" asked Florence.

"YOU!" snorted the sisters, "YOU can sing? Go on then, sing us a song right now!"

Florence took
a deep breath, raised
her head and opened her little
snout. But as she looked up, she saw
her big sisters peering down at her. Suddenly,
she felt very small, and very, very shy, and very, very,
very nervous. And all she could manage was a teeny, tiny . . .

"Squeak!"

Her sisters
burst out laughing.
"You can't sing with
us in the competition.
You can't even sing!"

Florence was so sad.

Every day she asked her sisters if she could join their singing practice, but every day they said

"No."

All Florence could do was listen to them rehearse. Soon she knew all the words front to back and back to front and inside out.

Finally the day of the competition arrived . . .

TELEVISION STUDIOS

The queue outside the television studios
stretched for miles and miles.

At last the doors opened, and the first band played their song. The judges looked impressed and the crowd cheered. Florence waited excitedly for her sisters to appear...

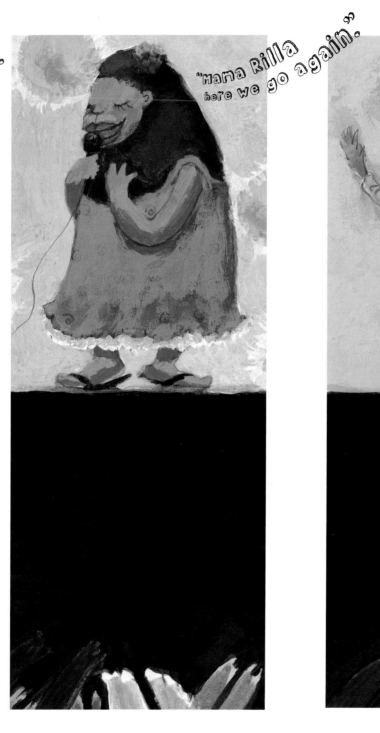

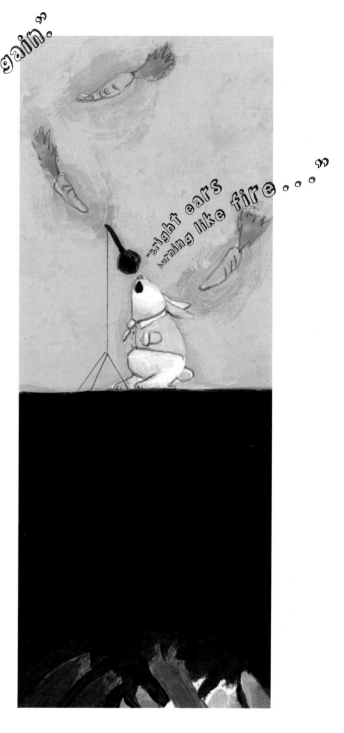

She waited and waited...

and waited...

and waited some more...

until finally...

Florence's sisters burst
onto the stage singing
with all their might. But as
they sang they looked out into the . . .

large crowd
and they started to feel
very small.
Then they looked up and saw the

TV cameras.
And they suddenly felt
very, very shy. And when
their eyes met with the . . .

beady eyes of the judges
they felt so nervous they forgot
all the words to their song!
Everything went quiet . . .

until a small voice started
singing from the crowd.
"Find that voice!"
shouted the judges.

The search-light went out over
the crowd, and guess who it found?

A small pink pig standing on
tip-toe, now singing with all her might!

"Please take to the stage,
little pig!" called the judges.

Florence's sisters were
not laughing at her now.

And as she trotted up to the stage,
Florence did not feel small, or shy or nervous.

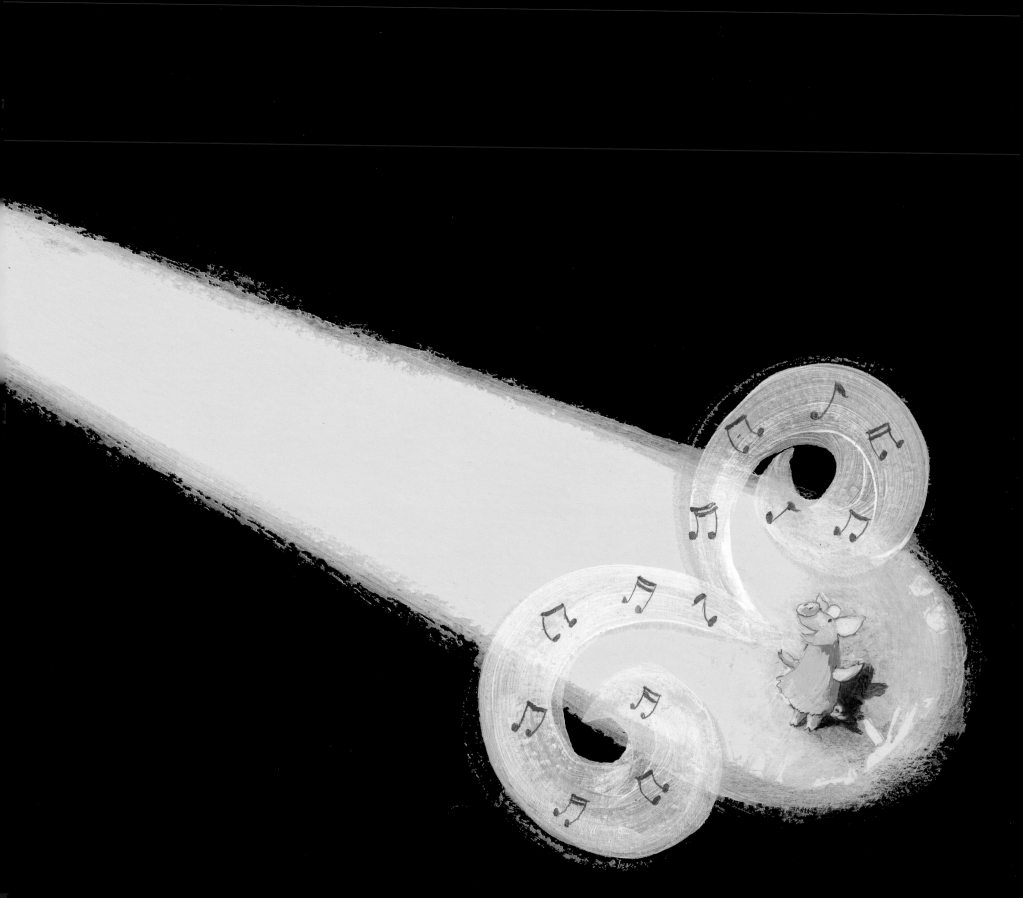

Florence was awarded First Prize.
And her dream of becoming a
piggy pop star was about to come true.

Florence topped the charts with songs about love, life and vegetarianism. And as for her sisters, they never sang again, but they made sure all their friends knew just who their little sister was!

"That's our sister."

"we taught her everything she knows!"

Other Gullane Children's Books
for you to enjoy . . .

Tabitha's Terrifically Tough Tooth

Charlotte Middleton

Lucy and the Bully

Claire Alexander

**Blame it on the Great
Blue Panda!**

Claire Freedman

Illustrated by

Emma Carlow & Trevor Dickinson

The Lamb-a-roo

Diana Kimpton

Illustrated by

Rosalind Beardshaw

Holly's Red Boots

Francesca Chessa